Under the Sea

Issue 10

Edited by Isabelle Kenyon

First published July 2022 by Fly on the Wall Press
Published in the UK by
Fly on the Wall Press
56 High Lea Rd
New Mills
Derbyshire
SK22 3DP

www.flyonthewallpress.co.uk
ISBN:978-1-913211-97-4

Edited by Isabelle Kenyon. Typesetting by Isabelle Kenyon. Cover photo Diana Saunders.

A CIP Catalogue record for this book is available from the British Library.

Contents

Rottingdean
Helen Kennedy

There's a body lying on the groyne
wrapped in bladder wrack—difficult to sex.
The sea drags at the rim of gravel as
I walk along the under cliff, check out the tide line.
Sometimes our identity is transitory,
exposed to the elements.
returned from the sea.

I gave up sex for years, the intertidal ebb and flow of motherhood.

The tide breathes in and out
I reclaimed myself
at the mid-life low water mark.
Women's bodies were soft like sugar kelp,
adapted to live on exposed shores.
Bioluminescent breasts
and hollow limbs grown on shells.

You came to Rottingdean to find me. But I'd already floated away, swum in moonlit high tides.
The sea constantly shifting.

Hawthorn Hive
Satterday Shaw

They used to send the coal dust from the pit to the edge of the cliff on a conveyor belt and tip it into the sea. The beach was black. The sea was black. They used to make glass in a factory before the end of days. Gobs and nuggets wash up and glisten blue or green.

Wild garlic and dog's mercury poke through. Snowdrops blossom through the pale, dead grass.

X and Y are picking up bricks, orange, terracotta, pink, black and yellow. X loves the different colours, Y loves the rounded shapes. The whippet clamps her teeth on a seaweed root and shakes it to and fro. If it were a baby rabbit she would break its neck. She lets it go so that it flies up, she chases after it. X and Y sing together. The sea is vast and grey. It breathes. It sucks and knocks the shingle.

Under the sea they are burning sea coal in the drowned villages. Getters and hewers with their pickaxes, hurriers and thrusters with their tubs, trappers and pit ponies. They are all gone, all gone under the sea. Under the sea they hang their ears and necks with marbles, multis and fisheyes. Glassblowers and blowers' dogs, all under the sea. The tide has washed them away.

The Weight of Water
Zoë Green

No accounting for the physiology of it, but lying prone in the water with a mask stuck to her face, she couldn't cry—as if the mask sealed the tears in. As if the Red Sea had already saltwater enough. 'It's impossible to be unhappy snorkeling,' Steve had said that morning, 'right?', a shadow of desperation in his voice, the skin pegged between his brows. How he'd like her to be happy—though a snarky part of her wondered if that was for his own sake rather than hers.

A shoal of little white fish with turquoise stripes passed like TV static. Lumps of brain coral lolled on the seafloor next to other cabbage-like corals. Sea cucumbers, black and marbled with white barnacles, lay comatose on the sand. Plastic danced on the sea floor: dispenser cups, cheese tubs, yoghurt pots. She flinched as a string of toilet roll hung suspended in the water in front of her. It was hard to see through the mask because her hair had got stuck in the seal and saltwater kept rushing in, stinging her eyes; it was only as she turned away that she realized that the strip of loo roll was actually a white-spotted moray-eel. Her heart sped up and adrenaline washed her lower stomach: it should be lurking in a cave at this time of day, which meant it had been disturbed, which meant it might bite. This was why she didn't like the ocean: things came out of the weight of water and the darkness, and bit you.

She paddled, arms by her sides. The water was, as Miriam had put it in her typically crude way, 'piss-warm'. As she'd set off from shore, Miriam had gestured vaguely in the direction of the rocks: 'The caves are over there, Laura. We'll get our kit on, then dive to twenty-five metres, then join you at the caves. Okay?'

Here she was. Here her husband and Miriam were not.

They'd driven to the Red Sea three days before, the van the only vehicle on the highway through the Negev, it being Shabbat. It was the first time Laura had met Miriam. She knew of her from social media where Steve and Miriam shared diving photos. Back in university, Steve had once dated a close friend of Miriam's. At the traffic junction in Jerusalem, just before they got into Miriam's van, Steve had said 'I can't promise Miriam will be nice'—whatever the hell that meant, but there hadn't been time to ask.

In the desert, they passed the desolate, jagged structures of officer barracks.

'I trained there,' Miriam said, and began a monologue about her military training; about how her dream was to free-dive to sixty metres; how she preferred this way from Jerusalem to Eilat than the Dead Sea Route, because the latter involved entering the Territories and she didn't believe Israel should be in the Territories. As she drove, dark curls lifting in the wind, she dispensed recipes for shakshouka, Israeli salad, limonana. Laura quite liked her that morning: she liked most people when they were new—like she liked a new pair of shoes that quickly became scuffed.

'We'll get Laura diving,' Miriam declared with a grin, as they caught a first glimpse of the red mountains of Jordan.

'Nah, I'm a land animal.'

'It's not difficult to dive. In truth, it's not logical to be afraid.'

Laura took a swig of water. It was warmer than the inside of her mouth. 'That's the point of phobias: they're not logical,' she said, voice neutral. So much dust flying in through the windows! Steve and Miriam were in the front, and she was in the back. Mom and Dad had decided she'd go diving, had they?

'I keep telling Laura she should try,' said Steve.

Miriam smiled a secret parental smile. 'Well, the truth is, we can't make her, can we?'

'I'll read, snorkel, walk along the beach. You two enjoy yourselves.'

Miriam, staring at the road ahead, spoke over her: 'Diving is a way of being free. Like driving a car, or riding a horse. Hey—how about you snorkel at Dolphin Beach?'

Steve reached his hand back as if to touch her knee, then dropped it back onto his lap. 'We could snorkel together,' he said.

A neon splash of happiness in her heart: 'I'd love to!'

'I mean, for me,' Miriam said, though nobody had asked her, 'dolphins are the Labradors of the sea world. But for tourists, it's a magical experience, for sure, yeah, totally.'

The first day Steve and Miriam dived and it was totally fine, and Laura even took a picture of them arm in arm, grinning in their wetsuits, their damp hair sticking to their shining wet skins. Anyone would have thought *they* were the couple. A waitress in a café asked if Miriam and Laura were sisters.   'She's too pretty to be my sister,' said Miriam, as if pretty were bad.

The light was very bright and reading proved tiring. Steve wasn't there to apply sunscreen so she burnt; by six o'clock a headache knitted the bones of her skull together and she went to bed shortly after. Steve and Miriam stayed out at a bar on the beach. When he came in, he slept on the sofa; he said next morning that it was because he hadn't wanted to disturb her. She thought of saying she wouldn't have minded if he had, but didn't.

That second day, her skin shrank tight and hot. Quarter past ten, they'd said they'd meet her after their first dive. But they didn't. For a while she imagined they'd drowned; Miriam could swim to forty without oxygen; if anyone had drowned, it would be Steve. It would be complicated flying the body home. Laura would have to tell his parents, and his father had a heart problem: maybe he'd suffer a second attack. She could make her mind go on anxious revolutions like this, working herself into hysteria; that was why they'd come on holiday—for her to relax and get out of her head.

Ten forty-five and they didn't emerge. Laura left her sun-lounger with her towel, pink as her skin, lying across it, and went up to the dive school in case she'd missed them. When she returned, they were side by side on her scuffed lounger. Three words exploded in Laura's head. Smug. Satiated. Strangers. She tasted blood on her tongue.

'Oh, there she is. We were wondering where you'd got to.' As if she was the one who was late. Miriam and Steve had both changed into matching white t-shirts that showed off their catalogue-perfect tans.

'Wow, you're really pink,' said Miriam. 'That's got to be painful.'

'Snorkel with me? Now?' she asked Steve, blocking Miriam out with her body.

Steve looked down at his clean, pressed t-shirt. 'I've just showered. I didn't bring my trunks.' The feeling of falling: he'd never intended to snorkel with her, or he'd forgotten.

Inhale for four, exhale for eight. *Relax.* 'How about Dolphin Beach?' she asked Miriam, hands on hips.

Lunch was early so that Steve and Miriam could fit in another dive. Laura ate a quinoa salad.

'The food is so healthy here,' she said, to show herself she was trying.

'Yeah,' said Miriam, 'Israelis eat very healthily. Brits talk about "five a day"; when I first heard that, I though that meant just for breakfast, not for the whole day!' She kept her mouth wide open after she'd finished laughing and Laura was reminded of a shark letting fish swim into its mouth.

'Oh, hey, I'll call the dolphin place now,' said Miriam. She turned away, holding the phone to her ear with both hands. Laura couldn't hear the conversation over the din of knives and forks and pop music and an espresso machine. Miriam ended the call and made a tschuking sound: 'They're booked up till we leave. Bad timing, unfortunately.'

Laura saw that Steve was busy reading the pudding menu and hadn't even heard that the dolphin place was full. If Miriam had bothered to book on the first day! If she'd thought about Laura for even a moment! She arranged granules of spilt salt and pepper into a little pile in front of her, then drew her finger once decisively through it.

All day she waited for Miriam to say something like: 'You two lovebirds go and have some time together.' But Miriam was never not there, except when she was not there at the same time that Steve was not there.

Only that night did Laura have her husband to herself. She showered in the youth hostel shower and covered her body in shea butter; donned a white nightshirt. The butter made her legs soft and slippery like eels. When she returned to the room the light was off. When she tried to kiss Steve awake, he turned his head away.

'Don't do that.'

She curled her body around his.

'You're making me hot. Your body's so hot.'

'I want to go snorkeling with you tomorrow.'

He opened an eye: 'All okay?'

'You know, I'd like some time with you.'

He closed his eyes and sighed: 'Look, Miriam took three days off work to drive us down here. She's a diver. And I'm a diver. And you don't dive. But I thought you were enjoying yourself. I thought you liked Miriam.' She sensed him frowning in the dark. 'You're doing a lot of waiting around. Maybe you should have stayed in Jerusalem.'

'I want to snorkel with the dolphins.'

There was a tight silence before he said, 'I'll speak with Miriam in the morning. Maybe we can all go to the same place in the water, and you snorkel and we dive. How 'bout that?'

Her heart lifted. She should have said something earlier. All this anxiety over nothing! He was right: she was too much in her head.

Miriam had said they'd reach the caves—where she and Steve could dive, and Laura could snorkel —twenty minutes after entering the water. But Laura—tired of watching as they stretched on their neoprene suits, shouldered the silver cylinders, adjusted weight belts and checked gauges—didn't know when exactly they'd entered the water. She couldn't see any caves. Rocks, sure. Where had

Miriam meant her to go? The waves came in bigger, splashing over her snorkel so she inhaled brine. She trod water, emptying the snorkel, then paddled round the group of rocks a second time. A school of lapis-blue damsel fish swam by, looking as if they should hang from a child's mobile. Fat green and purple parrot fish nuzzled the rocks, and a black clown coris with a green cummerbund shimmied past. *It's impossible to be unhappy when snorkeling.* Yeah, right, Steve. The guy who thought he could always will everything to be okay. Out of the gloom, she caught two silver stripes: a pair of divers. Her heart quickened. The divers held hands. She wondered if it was protocol to hold hands with your buddy. She couldn't see what colour their hair was, whether it was her husband's blond curls and his university friend's dark curls. On balance, she didn't think it was them. She swam on.

Her body felt weak against the waves. Shore was far off, with sunbathers the size of raisins. She began a panicked front crawl back. Way below, the current tugged a piece of yellow seaweed to and fro. It was a hand waving. Miriam's toad-like face under a mask. Her husband swimming out from a crack between the rocks behind her. He was waving too. All that weight of water between them. She waved back. Waited for them to come up and join her. When they breathed, fountains of silver bubbles glittered upwards and prickled her belly. She floated face down, hands and legs akimbo. Steve turned on his back, mirroring her. All that water, tons and tons, between them. Then he flipped onto his stomach and waved once more before following Miriam into the gloom between the rocks. They were gone, and she was alone.

She couldn't leave the water straightaway because, in the only section of the beach that wasn't roped off to protect the coral, a school of divers was hovering just beneath the surface. When she did eventually wade out, she found the van locked, her towel and dry clothes and book shut inside. Likely Miriam had the key strapped to her wetsuit in some special sealed IDF packet.

Laura sat on the beach, feet in the water, and shivered in the northerly wind. The sea, in which Israel, Egypt and Jordan met, looked black in the sun. Her husband and his friend were out there together somewhere. A dog wearing a tatty red collar stood hock-deep in the waves and watched her. When it tried to get out, she saw its hind legs were crippled, and she began to cry, hugging her body. She wasn't allowed to believe in these stories in which the handsome strong prince came along and saved the day: she was supposed to save herself, wasn't she? And yet, there was no doubt that both she and the dog needed rescuing. Watching the dog's futile scrabbling, watching the dark surface of the sea, she knew suddenly that it was less about her getting out of her head and more about needing to feel Steve's arms around her, lifting her, responding to her, in the way he used to. They'd promised, in their wedding vows, hadn't they—that each would lift the other up? She pushed herself to her feet, walked down to the dog, and staggered under its wet weight as she carried it to the beach, where it lay panting in the sun next to her. She rested her hand on the its head and rehearsed how she'd speak to Steve when he finally got back in. She had to make sure he heard this time.

Seafood Buffet
Hannah Brown

I am drifting in the swell of the under-wave like a piece of lonely, corrugated seaweed. My hair ripples out around me in a cloud of red fire dimmed and made dark by the waves. Fish worry past me, teasing my shrivelled fingertips and dropping little kisses on my arms, legs, hips.

Overhead I hear the steady chug of a boat's engine. I wonder if it will come to disturb my rest. It has been so long since I had any visitors without gills. The boat overhead burbles to a stop, a distant pop of a champagne bottle, laughter, shrieking.

Splashes.

They disturb me, dragging down great funnels of bubbles that cause me to sway sickeningly back and forth. My ankle is caught still, wrapped in chain so tight and weighed down by the breeze blocks tied to the other end. A fear of discovery.

I watch with glassy eyes as they bob so easily back to the surface. A surface I barely remember; only the faint bright smudge of the sun filters down through miles of inky water. The fish hide; I am the only bipedal they know not to fear. Still, they will not find me here. They are no scuba divers. They are safe.

And so I drift, expecting sleep to find me again.

Anchor. The impact jars the ocean floor like an earthquake, shaking loose debris better forgotten. My breeze block slips loose, the chain scraping over the rocks and crunching under the strain of rust and friction and momentum.

I am free.

I float, like I never forgot how, drifting towards the surface like a promise of retribution. Those who sealed me down here are long gone now. None as longevous as I.

I crest the waves in a sop of wet red hair, push water out of my long-dormant lungs and cry in my prettiest voice.

'Help me!'

The humans are silent for only a moment before they rush to my aid, pulling me up onto their luxury boat, worried by my sudden appearance. Someone rallies to call the coast guard.

Playing the role of ingenue perfectly, I cast around for an imaginary boat. Hiding my sharp teeth as I say, 'Did you see them? The man who threw me in, did you see him?'

They gather around me, draping me in a towel as strength returns to my bones. They are beautiful, tall, strong and tan. Used to a life of luxury; a perfect first meal after a long rest.

They mobilize like toy soldiers, moving me further into their fort of protection. The women fuss, the coastguard is coming. Time is ticking down but I am faster than any boat. One girl, younger than the others, an ugly duckling in her knee-length shorts and awkward frizz of hair, watches me with guarded eyes. A likeness.

She knows. Some humans, ones used to being preyed on by their own kind, come to recognize predators of any sort. Her mind piecing together my puzzle pieces; long finger nails, ragged clothes, eyes too bright, cheeks too pink, stance too… dangerous.

A man touches my neck, titling my head back and flashing a sharp light into my eyes that burns my retina, so unaccustomed to the light.

A doctor, then. Who notices the way my pupils react to the light.

The first to go.

I tear into his neck with a suddenness that leaves the air sharp with breathless anticipation. A silence that hangs precariously for a second, waiting to be cut. The crack of a scream echoes soon after as blood rushes from his strong neck and oozes into my stomach. I tear muscle from bone, swallowing whole chunks of flesh as the deck descends into chaos. I drop him, wriggling like a gutted fish and turn, my chin a stain of bright red viscera, seeking out my next target.

A symphony of screams rends the air. They scramble away, some throwing themselves overboard, some running to lock themselves inside the cabin, one brave soul even tries to apprehend me. How pretty he looks as I tear the arms from his body and slurp out his tendons. Those in the water can wait; they will never out-swim me.

They plead as I yank the door from its hinges. They beg harder as I rip them limb from limb. The women I kill quickly, a hunter with morals, but the men I play with.

The deck is awash with a thick foam of crimson by the time I am finished. I sit opposite the ugly duckling, holding in my hand a grown man's still quivering heart.

She has not moved, locking down her muscles and staring at me, wide eyed. Horror has turned her face to stone that slowly cracks and shifts to curiosity as the seconds tick by. A mirror of myself, plucked exactly from my memory.

Monster that I am, I have not forgotten. I hold out the valentine's morsel to her.

'Bon appetit.'

Grandfather Salamander Resists Eviction
Sarah Wallis

Swim of living fossil, some grandfather
of the underworld, a lazy Mafiosi, blinking
at intrusion under the scuba mission light,
feels vibrations from the talking fish mask,
mer-curious in his house—
and doesn't like rude light, don't they know
it's twilight time in the sea gardens?

A heart floats by, formed of mating seahorses.

We're a dour sort, bottled green and wattle
daub, we like our mud, skin curious black
and pink rock stars of our world, the cousins
falling habitat—taken by dam—and you might
build us out, an artificial bunker but it doesn't
hold the dark like the mud and the weed,
it doesn't sway its walls with the music of the sea
and frankly, as the surveyor, I don't like what I see.

Endurance
Lorraine Carey

Endurance was the name it had to be.
In bell clear water this sunken wreck
destined for the depths of the Weddell Sea.

Rigging lay in a tangled spree
as anemones danced on the ghostly deck,
Endurance was the name it had to be.

Over the wooden stern you can clearly see
its brass name arced in glorious flecks
destined for the depths of the Weddell Sea.

The timber preserved and parasite free,
as subzero temperatures had little effect
Endurance was the name it had to be.

Shackleton saved his crew, helped them flee
bequeathed his ship with a captain's respect
destined for the depths of the Weddell Sea,

she remains undisturbed and forever at peace.
Encountering extremes of an Antarctic trek
the submersible struck gold at ten thousand feet,
Endurance was the name it had to be.

Mereswine

Baltic Harbour Porpoise

Gerry Stewart

Herring once ran these waters
and we were mercury quick
beside the silver darlings,
rolling and tumbling with the joy of it.

The sea's banquet now stripped clean,
trawling beyond recovery.
We chase poisoned scraps,
their siren's call entangling us in greed.

Ghost nets hover with weedy fingers,
our echoes brushing past them,
yet they pull us down beneath the currents
far from our blessed draught of air.

Invisible boundaries cannot repair hindsight,
though we swim alone
we hear through the deep
the ticking pulse
of our eventual vanishing.

Breeching Whale
Gerry Stewart

Our songs echo beneath the surface,
reaching outwith our ken.
You cannot hear how I revel
in the current slick over my skin,
how I await the burst of air,
launching past the extra pull of gravity
if only for a second.

So obsessed with your horizon,
what your eyes expose,
your do not feel the pulse
of the world's depths
vibrating.

We do not dance for you,
but from our joy
of being one with the sea,
a part of its pull and power
and in the hope that some day
you will understand.

Whispers to the Baltic Sea
Gerry Stewart

Why so silent?

Why do your waves
not sing?

Other seas
tuck their salt into our mouths,
shout their charms
and splash about.

Your stories
are held deep,
colder than black,
blacker than cold.

I skim your surface
like a shining stone.

Summers dance in light
or dressed in mist,
your winter sleep
is scaled with ice.

Laugh to the wind,
roll beneath
the wide basket of sky.

Speak the ache of storms,
the pounding rage
of climate change,
the fade
of your porpoise swift,
algae's blue-green
menacing drift.

Grant me your cold kiss,
make my skin
glisten.

Listen.
Your cry
is a song we share.

Itämeri,
Baltic blue,
I hear you.

Becoming Krill
Rupert Locke

first I learnt to breathe
in different places
those who saw the gills
spill from my carapace
tried to tease them off

soon every frame widened
I'd catch at certain glances
up and down my body
the bars of a gas fire
thumped into flame

my self shrank to inches
she didn't seem to mind
grabbing me at night
her net of swimmerets
raking up to mine

till leviathan arrived—
the feeding frenzy started
I saw then we were small fry
salty little punches
made for other mouths

Mermaids

(After *'The Legend of the Padstow Doombar'* by Enys Tregarthen)

Rupert Locke

Hair the colour of oats you said
Waiting for the sickle

All glammed up with nowhere to go
Sat on a rock at Hawker's Cove

Police appeal for information
Searchers face extreme conditions

All glammed up with nowhere to go
Sat on a rock at Hawker's Cove

A dresser, a settle, a chestful of linen
A mermaid crowns a Cornish kitchen

All glammed up with nowhere to go
Sat on a rock at Hawker's Cove

Higher St. Saviour's cordoned off
Man arrested, pleads bewitchment

All glammed up with nowhere to go
Sat on a rock at Hawker's Cove

A bar of sand dooms the town
The masts and spars, the lifeless drowned

All glammed up with nowhere to go
Sat on a rock at Hawker's Cove

Yes all the poor sailors, sent to their deaths
(One sea-green comb, one seaweed dress)

All glammed up with nowhere to go
Sat on a rock at Hawker's Cove

Spike
Kathryn O'Driscoll

Skeletal swimmer,
headless, parting kelp strands
that tickle on bone.
Sea urchin for a heart;
clasped by clam stone fist
it rolls through the current
clattering its needles
against small fish, debris,
longing looks, refracting,
and someone else's breath
in a net of bubblework.
Joints knotted together
with frayed rope and other
pollutants stolen from sand.
A mere mercalamity
holding tight to the shape
of a person whilst the waves
tug. Trying to unspool every
thing.

I remember when the sea swelled up to my door
Marcelle Newbold

when I thought
it would tip right in
        that a boundary would be broken
        that all that darkness would stain
        that I would never be dry again
        that the liquid would become ingrained.
I remember when I wished
it would slosh all around me
        hoped the colours would bleed
        hoped for an engulfing
        hoped for the taste of brine
        hoped I could not swim
believed it was here for me.

Only Home
Carl Alexandersson

i.

we almost trip
>on the washed-up jellyfish

as we walk into the ocean;
>two modern-day selkies returning

home. the waves swallowing
>us, on a straight path downwards. we are acting

as if we could steer away from this path
>at any time, to explore the shipwrecks and crevices

and meadows of algae we pass by
>as if we are not the passers-by of this world.

ii.

two men holding hands
>are passers-by of many worlds;

driftwood thrown out to sink again. but look,
>we breathe as well here as elsewhere. and look,

there might be others down here;
>jellyfish or selkies or remains, even

the oceans of ourselves *do* remain largely unexplored,
>all waves and foam and surfaces—

iii.

the darker it gets the more we feel
      the presence of others. as in,

we might never get to *see*
      the bottom of the ocean, but

we can still let it
      swallow us.

iv.

the pressure here might kill us,
      my love. match it with your hand—

we only dissolve
      if we stop walking.

v.

we

        are

  only

      home

      when we say we are.

Siren Song
Cheryl Byrne

The sand was sharp against her soles, each step scraping. She breathed in the salt on the night air, let it fill her lungs, infuse her blood. She liked to imagine tiny sea salt crystals scouring her clean from the inside as it travelled to her fingers and toes. Scrubbing away the stresses of life and the funk of travel. She reached the waves and let her feet sink into the sand until she was buried to her ankles, the cold water lapping at her calves shocking and comforting. She closed her eyes and listened for the song under the rushing of the waves.

The ache across her shoulders hadn't entirely left her yet. Every time she had been here before, the song had been there almost as soon as she entered the house, massaging her, dissolving all the kinks and tightness. This time, she had been there for nearly an hour and nothing. She hadn't realised what was wrong at first.

"Does something seem off?" she had asked Dylan, as she padded over the chill of the tiles, picking up the blue and red porcelain shells on top of the book shelf.

"How would I know? This is my first time," he replied, with a little shortness that could be forgiven after a long journey. He followed her into the kitchen, watched her finger the yellow plastic flower on the table. "There isn't a smell or anything?" he asked.

"No. No, it must be my imagination," she replied. When Dylan opened the door and the sound of the waves filled the room, she realised what it was. "I'm going to the beach for a walk," she told him.

Her body hummed for the want of it, as though it could call the sea's song to her with its own music. It started, finally, soon after she reached the waves, after the water touched her skin, like it was awoken by the taste of her. It was a song of longing and belonging. Its notes soothed and excited her. It was hers. She breathed in a long deep breath and smiled. The last ache in her shoulders was carried away and she swayed slowly in time with the rhythm and the waves.

The first time she had heard it, she had been thirteen. Their first trip here after her parents had bought the house. Her Dad had lived in Italy when he was young and had dreams of returning. A holiday home by the sea was the first step to that. They hadn't gotten much past the first step.

"Where's that music coming from?" she had asked, her half-formed face turned this way and that in search of a source.

"What music?" her mother had asked looking up from her sand scattered towel, a crime thriller held limply in one hand.

"That song, can't you hear it? It's been playing since we got here."

"Your discman is probably still running, check your headphones," she replied her eyebrows crinkling behind her sunglasses and she went back to her book.

"No, it can't be that. It's been going since last night, and it isn't like anything I have."

Her mother nodded but didn't look up. Lyra mentioned it again that night, and a few more times on that first trip. But she soon learned to stop as her curiosity was rebuffed by exasperated looks and orders to stop being silly. She kept it to herself. A strange musical secret that she relished and worried about sharing, worried about people finding out.

That year, she learned about Sirens. Women who sang songs at sea to lure people to their death. It didn't frighten her. The voices of these women were only a danger to men in the stories.

And the song she heard wasn't insistent, didn't attempt to lure her. It was more like it was letting her know it was there. Waiting for when she was ready.

"Lyra," Dylan called from the garden, his voice out of tune.

"Over here," she called back.

He made his way toward her, his breath loud and off beat. "What are you doing?" he asked as he reached her, standing a little behind.

"Just saying hello to the sea," she said, turning to face him. He still had his trainers on and his jeans.

"To the sea?" he asked, brushing a hand over his shaved head and laughing gently. "Did it have anything to say back?"

She smiled and pulled her feet from the sand reaching for his hand and they made their way back to the house.

They occupied themselves with the little domesticities of settling in to a long holiday. Unpacking, finding places for all their clothes and arranging toothbrushes in the bathroom. Lyra had been here so often it was automatic, she knew where the best place to plug in her phone was and the way that you had to push the tap slightly after having a shower to stop that last little trickle of water.

"I didn't know you were so into the sea," Dylan said taking a dish filled with pasta from the fridge. Their neighbour Mathilde had left it there for them and Lyra made a note to invite her for dinner soon to say thank you.

"You haven't ever seen me by the sea."

"I guess," he put the dish in the oven and turned to take plates out of the cupboard. The clinking of the cutlery was a discordant percussion for the song. Lyra opened a bottle of wine. "You just... seem different."

"I'm relaxed," she shrugged and sat at the table, "I think this might be the only place I'm ever really relaxed."

Lyra took a sip of the wine, red and slightly sweet. It lacked the hint of bitterness of most wines in England. She enjoyed sitting back whilst Dylan served her dinner. She didn't offer to help, and he didn't ask. He just passed her a plate piled with pasta coated lightly in a fresh tomato sauce. She stabbed the swirls with her fork and shovelled it in to her mouth.

"Mathilde is a genius," she said through her mouthful of food. It was sharp and fresh, tingling on her tongue as she chewed.

That night, Dylan fell asleep quickly, breathing long and deep breaths just this side of snoring. Lyra lay on her side looking through the gap in the yellow curtains at a glimpse of the sea. Her fingers twitched with the energy of it, but soon the song lulled her.

They went to the beach the next day. Laid out towels and bottles of water and books. They lay on the sand and the sun warmed their skin. Lyra looked out to the sea while Dylan read next to her, his hand draped over her leg, his thumb absently stroking her thigh. She stared out into the horizon. The boundlessness of it thrilled and terrified her and she couldn't help wondering what life would be like without walls. Only the waves and the openness and the song around her.

"I'm going for a swim," Dylan said patting her thigh lightly before standing.

"Ok," Lyra said and watched him walk down to the water. He waded in until he was waist deep and then dove. His arms reached over his head one after the other, scooping the water. From where Lyra sat, it looked as if he was fighting the waves, seeking to subdue them. The sea sang on, oblivious to his efforts. She longed to follow him, show him that he should work with the waves, with the rhythm of the song and let them support him through the motions. But she hadn't quite gotten there yet. Hadn't been able to let herself go to the sea in that way. She would be almost there, on the edge of embracing it, but the limitlessness of it stopped her, made the loss of control feel impossible.

She stood and walked into the sea until it reached her chest. The song became louder, encouraged her whilst the waves pushed at her. It urged her to let herself relax into it. The water moved the sand beneath her feet and soon they were buried in it. Dylan swam to her, stood in front of her. He put his arms around her and kissed her and said, "I'm glad we came here."

"Me too," she replied and laid her head against his chest. The song quietened.

Mathilde knocked at the door exactly on time. She breezed into the room, wearing cream palazzo pants and a floaty blue blouse. She swooped on Lyra like an elegant bird, kissing her, lips smooth and firm against her cheek. Dylan followed her into the kitchen, his steps plodding and awkward, like a seal on land compared to Mathilde, a dolphin jumping effortlessly in the waves.

"My love, how are you? It's been too long," she said and her words held music in them, each syllable blending into the song, flowing around the notes and harmonising with it. Not for the first time, Lyra wondered whether Mathilde could hear it too.

Dylan poured her some wine, spilling a little on the table, the red drops bled into the white of the table cloth.

"Thank you, Dylan," Mathilde said as he handed her the glass, she wiped away the red drop hanging from the base. His name in her mouth was strange, like she was talking about someone Lyra didn't know.

"How long have you lived here Mathilde?" Dylan asked and Lyra was struck by the contrast of his voice with hers. Where hers ebbed and flowed, his was all sharp vowels and hard edges.

"All my life," she replied. "Lyra and I played in the sea as children. I don't remember a time when I couldn't hear the music from the waves."

They ate gnocchi and drank wine and they caught up in that way of old friends. Dylan listened contently, adding a question here and there, pleased to learn more about Lyra's teenage years. When they had finished the last glass and Dylan had gone to bed, Mathilde and Lyra sat in the garden in silence for a while. Lyra watched her, the way that she held her head, tilted slightly and her eyes closed.

"This is the first man you have brought here," Mathilde said.

"Yes."

"He must be important to you."

"Maybe, I think he could be."

Later, Dylan lay on top of her, his breath loud in her ears. She became confused in the competing rhythms, first moving in time with him, then with the song. They were more out of sync than usual, a mess of accidental hair pulling and bumped teeth. After, she lay in his arms and he pulled her tighter to him, pressing her against his side. The noises of his body; panting, heartbeat, the murmur of contentment, for a moment, blocked the song from the sea. She sat up quickly.

"Are you ok?" he asked as she pulled her dress over her head and mumbled something about needing a drink.

Barefoot, she walked over the beach, not stopping at the waves, she waded in. Her dress floated around her, the red flowers looked black in the dark. The song had come back almost straight away and in the water, it grew louder and she drew it to her, pulled it inside her with urgency. She steadied as it filled her, the panic draining away. The song was essential. She belonged to it and it to her. The noises of her body, the hum of her blood filled the spaces between the notes. A wave rushed toward her and she let it take her, pull her down and up, and then she danced with the sea. Swayed with the surf. The song beneath the waves embraced her, its arms felt natural around her. She sang with the song.

The Price of Freedom
Eleonora Balsano

I was born at the bottom of the ocean, and there I will die.

A king's daughter, murdered by a king's son, a man who sailed the seven seas, yet he's afraid of depths.

I didn't know the word for light, I never needed it in the deep. My father made me out of sand and poured seafoam through my veins. Eels rocked me to sleep in the faint glow of jellyfish and seahorses nibbled at my toes in the morning, gently bringing me back from my dreams. I wore starfish around my neck and a coral tiara on top of my head. Orcas ferried me around, sharks guarded my quarters. I now reckon I had everything, yet something always seemed to be missing.

As I grew older, my world grew smaller. I asked jellyfish to stay away from my underwater cave. They weren't glowing miracles, as I used to believe. Just gelatinous monsters. I ripped all the starfish from my neck, irked by their suckers constantly tickling my skin, leaving red marks behind.

In my dreams, I ventured out of my father's kingdom, close to the surface, where elderly mermaids said fish were all the colours we couldn't see.

A day shy of my eighteenth birthday I distracted the sharks patrolling my cave and escaped. I swished my tail up and down, with all the strength I could muster, propelling myself to the surface.

Dozens of boats paraded before my eyes while hands clapped on the nearby shore. I had heard about people, but I had never seen them. They looked like they knew things we didn't. I swam to the shore and hid behind a rock. A man was standing on the bow of the first ship, wearing a rich costume and a sad smile. As he approached, dozens of other men kneeled in front of him.

I crawled on the beach and slept under the stars, dreamt of a life larger than the ocean.

The following morning, I woke to find my tail dry and itchy in the sun.

The forces of the ocean had granted me a wish upon my birth. I asked for legs.

I watched my scales turn to ashes. In their place, a pair of legs had grown, long and smooth and difficult to use at first.

As I staggered away, a seal approached me.

'Your wish has been granted but you need to give the ocean something back. There is no free gift in our world, and neither in this one, as you will find out, eventually,' he said.

'What do you want?' I asked, still unstable on my new feet.

'If you want to live with humans, then be it. But you will lose your voice. Its melody will stay at the bottom of the sea.'

'I understand,' I said, hearing my voice for the last time.

'It's not all,' he added. 'You'll walk, but not without pain. With every step, you'll remember this is not where you were born, or where you were supposed to live.'

Anything to be free, I thought, with the naivety of those who never had to mend a broken heart.

I danced my way into the grandest houses and palaces. At night, when I took my shoes off, my feet were reduced to morsels of raw, bloody flesh. I dressed them in clean gauze and waited for the skin to grow back before morning. Week after week, I danced and bled until I met the man from the boat again. He was the king's son and he said he'd never known bliss before he saw me.

We married on a moonlit night on the shore. My bare feet didn't bleed in the seawater. For some time, we were happy.

One day my husband asked me why I couldn't speak. He was growing tired of the notes I used to leave on his pillow in the morning.

'I'll find the best doctor in the kingdom for you,' he said.

I shook my head and wrote, *no doctor can ever heal my voice,* but my answer didn't satisfy him.

'I want to hear your voice,' he insisted. 'How will our children learn to speak with a mother like you?'

We didn't have any children yet. Every month, when blood crushed my hopes, I wondered if I hadn't sacrificed motherhood, too, alongside my voice and health.

My husband stopped visiting me at night. He sailed for weeks at a time and when he came back, he avoided being alone with me.

I followed him one night. He went to the theatre and sat in the first row, listening for hours to a woman singing with the voice of an angel, or of a mermaid still leaving at the bottom of the sea.

I saw him fall in love, with the quiet desperation of those who thought they would never know joy again. Before the winter winds disrobed the trees in our garden and covered our windows with frost, he left me.

'I can't grow old with a woman who's lost her voice,' he said.

'I gave it up for you. For you!' I screamed without sound.

'I need a woman who knows her worth and isn't afraid to ask for more,' he replied, as I melted into seafoam at his feet.

The Otter World
Elizabeth Gibson

In our world, which is a lot like yours, we can turn to otters.
We ease ourselves into our fur, scuttle into frothy waves,
raise babies on our domed bellies, then become people again.

This has been going on for centuries, you know, but recently,
with the increase in what we humans carry—clothes, bags,
shoes, keys, money, jewellery, books and papers and more—

the question rose, where does it go, when we take otter form?
Gradually, we realised it sits as extra weight beneath our fur,
a bit cumbersome but still ours, and in the winter months,

it keeps us full and warm. Once we slide back to human,
some of it stays settled beneath the skin, shaping and curving
our silhouettes, offering a glimpse of days navigating the tides,

depths and shallows, storms, cubs and fights, long dark nights.
When people observe your body, ask with their eyes, you say,
hey—I know, I am a bit fatter, but you see... I was an otter.

They never quite get it, so you are quiet, know your secret:
it doesn't matter who they knew, or thought they knew, then.
You are carved from the oceans, child: epic, transient. Here.

In the Deep-Sea Garden
Diana Sanders

In the deep-sea garden
time is different

No solstice, equinox,
dawn, sunset.

In pitch-black,
coral grows.

Squid weaves
between branches
tracing the blue
glow of a mate.
In the jaws of a fish,
a brittle star
casts off a trapped
flashing limb—

which re-forms
in the dark-garden.

Zombie sharks
fall from light
broken, finless—

creating feeding
frenzies in the deep.

Above, humans
spoon shark-fin soup
between their blood-red lips.

Celeste Scuro
Martina Bani

The afternoon light reminded me
of the smell of coming back
retreating
from the scorching beach
the look of foreign toilets
of the Adriatic riviera
the afternoon adventures, sitting
on an oddly-sheeted bed
with the remnants of the sand
stuck to the skin, easily flicked away
the light is *celeste scuro*
like the crayon colour I loved as a kid
I don't need to be strong like the waves, I can rest
I can smell the diesel of the return
and the pastel tables
the makeshift seats
and the homemade paninis
I can find refuge
in my mother holding me
she doesn't know the lyrics of *Aquarela*,
like my father,
but she hums it all the same.

Biographies (in order of appearance)

1. Helen Maire Kennedy is a Mancunian writer and playwright whose work has been performed by The Irish in London theatre (2019) and has been shortlisted for the Cambridge prize for Short Fiction and Flash Fiction (2021). She is currently undertaking an MA in Creative Writing in Oxford and working on her debut novel 'Blessed Women,' and her collection of Flash Fiction 'Manchester Fishing.'

2. The first in her family to attend university, Satterday Shaw has a PhD from Northumbria University in Creative Writing (conferred 2014). Her work has been printed in *Meniscus, Mslexia*, *The London Magazine,* a Chawton House anthology, *Wasafiri*, *The Yellow Room* and other publications.

3. Zoë Green is a Scottish writer who lives and works in Vienna and Berlin. She has been published in the London Magazine, Ink Sweat and Tears, Atrium, and Harpers and Queen.

4. Originally from Wales, Hannah Brown is a Tokyo-based writer currently studying for her MA in Creative Writing. You can find her on Twitter @Hannah_Aimee_17.

5. Sarah Wallis is a writer based in Scotland and has published work cross genre, in poetry, fiction, and for the stage. Highlights include inclusion in The Yorkshire Poetry Anthology, staging of her plays The Rain King and Laridae, and published chapbooks Medusa Retold with @fly_press, Precious Mettle @thealienbuddha and How to Love the Hat Thrower @ SelcouthStation. Contacts: sarahwallis.net & @wordweave on tw.

6. Lorraine Carey's poems are widely anthologised and published in Gyroscope Review, Allium, The High Window, Ink Sweat &Tears, Poetry Ireland Review, Bindweed, Orbis, Atrium, Prole, Poetry Birmingham, The Honest Ulsterman, Rust+Moth and Marble among others. Her paintings and photography have featured online in Barren, Olentangy Review and Three Drops From A Cauldron. A Pushcart nominee, she was runner up in Trocaire / Poetry Ireland and The Blue Nib Chapbook Competition in 2017 shortlisted for the Allingham Prize (2019, 2020 and 2021) and longlisted in The National Poetry Competition 2019. Her debut collection is From Doll House Windows (Revival).

7. Gerry Stewart is a poet, creative writing tutor and editor based in Finland. Her poetry collection Post-Holiday Blues was published by Flambard Press, UK. Totems is to be published by Hedgehog Poetry Press in 2022. Her writing blog can be found at http:// thistlewren.blogspot.fi/ and @grimalkingerry on Twitter.

8. Rupert Locke is a teacher and poet based in North Devon. His poetry has appeared in 'Picaroon', 'Nine Muses Poetry', 'Ink, Sweat and Tears', 'Sarasvati' and 'Fly on the Wall Press Magazine'. He has also appeared in two anthologies: 'Lost Things' by Reading Room Café Project Publishing, and 'Planet in Peril' by Fly on the Wall Press.

9. Kathryn O'Driscoll is a spoken word poet, writer and activist from Bath, England. She is a UK Slam Champion and a World Slam Finalist who talks openly about disabilities, mental health, neurodiversity, LGBTQIA+ issues and joys and gender politics in her wide range of poems. Her debut collection 'Cliff Notes' was published by Verve Poetry Press in February.

10. Marcelle Newbold's poetry explores place and inheritance. Pushcart Prize nominated, and

winner of the Poetry in the Arcades competition in 2020, her poems have been published in online and print magazines including Ink Sweat & Tears, Iamb poet, and The Ekphrastic Review. Her writing has featured in recent print anthologies by Black Bough Poetry, Maytree Press, Wild Pressed Books, Icefloe Press, and Indigo Dreams. Marcelle lives in Cardiff, Wales where she trained as an architect. Linktree: marcellenewbold

11. Carl Alexandersson (he/him) is a queer spoken word poet and writer, based in Edinburgh. He was selected for the BBC Words First programme in 2021, awarded the UniSlam Slambassadors Award in 2020, and a runner-up for the 2022 Grierson Verse Prize. His work has been published in *Atrium Poetry, Ink Sweat & Tears, Impossible Archetype,* and more.

12. Cheryl Byrne is a writer based in Manchester who primarily writes short stories. She is Head of Community for Orton Publishing and is involved in running events for their writing group, and collaborative projects. She is deeply obsessed with mythology, Italy and her yellow roller skates decorated with rainbows. Some of her previous work can be found in Analogies and Allegories and Fly on the Wall Magazine.

13. Eleonora Balsano (she/her) is an Italian-born, polyglot writer based in Brussels, E. U. Her short fiction has been published or is forthcoming in Fictive Dream, Reflex Fiction, Janus Literary, Micro Podcast and elsewhere. In 2021 she was shortlisted for the Bridport Prize. Eleonora is working on a dystopian novel. Tweets @norami. Website: eleonorabalsano.net

14. Elizabeth Gibson is a queer Manchester writer and performer. She has been the recipient of a Northern Writers' Award, and a DYCP grant from Arts Council England. Her writing has appeared in Mancunian Ways, as well as Atrium, Confingo, Lighthouse, Magma, Popshot, Queerlings, and Under the Radar. She is on Twitter and Instagram as @Grizonne.

15. Diana Sanders is a musician, composer and poet who lives and works in North Wales. She has had work published in the USA and the UK.

16. Martina Bani writes poetry that dwells on strokes of female experience, unorganised forms of beauty, and existential questioning in a dense layering of painted metaphors. She draws her intuitions from her background in film and philosophy at Oxford, Glasgow and Sydney. She usually sits uncomfortably between hubris and humblings.

About Fly on the Wall Press

A publisher with a conscience.
Publishing high quality anthologies on pressing issues, novels, short stories and poetry, from exceptional writers around the globe. Founded in 2018 by founding editor, Isabelle Kenyon.

Some other publications:

The Woman With An Owl Tattoo by Anne Walsh Donnelly
the sea refuses no river by Bethany Rivers
The Prettyboys of Gangster Town by Martin Grey
The Sound of the Earth Singing to Herself by Ricky Ray
Inherent by Lucia Orellana Damacela
Medusa Retold by Sarah Wallis
Pigskin by David Hartley
We Are All Somebody
Aftereffects by Jiye Lee
Someone Is Missing Me by Tina Tamsho-Thomas
Odd as F*ck by Anne Walsh Donnelly
Muscle and Mouth by Louise Finnigan
Modern Medicine by Lucy Hurst
These Mothers of Gods by Rachel Bower
Sin Is Due To Open In A Room Above Kitty's by Morag Anderson
Fauna by David Hartley
How To Bring Him Back by Clare HM
Hassan's Zoo and A Village in Winter by Ruth Brandt
No One Has Any Intention of Building A Wall by Ruth Brandt
The House with Two Letter-Boxes by Janet H Swinney
The Guts of a Mackerel by Clare Reddaway
A Dedication To Drwoning by Maeve McKenna
Man at Sea by Liam Bell
Cracked Asphalt by Sree Sen

Social Media:

@fly_press (Twitter) @flyonthewall_poetry (Instagram)
@flyonthewallpress (Facebook)
www.flyonthewallpress.co.uk